HIGHLAND VIEWS

DAVID ROSS

Published by Two Ravens Press
Green Willow Croft
Rhiroy
Loch Broom
Ullapool
Ross-shire IV23 2SF

www.tworavenspress.com

ISBN: 978-1-906120-05-4

British Library Cataloguing in Publication Data. A CIP record
for this book can be obtained from the British Library.

Designed and typeset by Two Ravens Press.
Cover design by David Knowles and Sharon Blackie.

Printed on Forest Stewardship Council-accredited paper by
Biddles Ltd., King's Lynn, Norfolk.

Biography

After completing a degree at Edinburgh University, David Ross stayed on in the capital for another fifteen years, working at a variety of jobs from lecturer to dish-washer. He wrote two draft novels and ran a Creative Writing Workshop for Theatre Workshop as well as playing and song-writing in several bands, including Poetry Roadshow, a words/music fusion of performance poets and musicians.

Returning to his home town of Tain in Easter Ross, he began writing *Highland Views* and worked mostly as a musician and tutor, initially with the Highlands Music Centre, and Invergordon Community Arts Project. He was later responsible for developing Music Performance and Sound Production courses for North Highland College in its Alness Centre, and a Creative Writing Course in Dornoch.

David Ross is currently self-employed as a guitar, composition and recording tutor.

Acknowledgments

The Seer was first published in *West Coast Magazine* Issue 24.

The Crash was first published in *Northwords* Issue 2.

A Lament For The Union was first published in *West Coast Magazine* Issue 11.

In fond memory of

my father

HIGHLAND VIEWS

THE SEER

The Seer

At a first glance his slowness might well be put down to old age, what with John that far on in his years, but it was no more than his own particular way of paying heed to what he was doing. However much time was left to him yet in his retirement, he could afford to let it pass a shade slower than the rest of it had gone in, and the little that needed doing these days still got done.

The breakfast dishes were washed and back in the cupboard, and the animals wouldn't need fed until later on, so he got the ladders down from their hooks in the garage rafters, ready for a couple of small jobs that had been waiting on the milder weather.

Aye, it was mild enough out that Monday morning, unusually mild for the first week in March, with a warming wind in over the hills from the west. And from the looks of it, the rain would surely hold off long enough for him to get the windows cleaned first of all. Soon the ladders had been propped up against the top sill, but then John stopped all of a sudden, as if some warning scent had caught in his nostrils. That was always the way it would start to come over him, and when John MacKenzie smelt something of that nature in the air, the years had long since taught him neither to worry it nor to ignore it.

Instead of climbing the ladders then, he walked down the garden path and stood with his back to the gate, searching his surroundings for anything that would be a mirror to the sober mood he found himself in. Around his feet there were yellow wedges starting to push the buds open on the daffodils, and the snowdrops and the crocuses were well on for the time of year. In the far corner of the garden there was even a faint haze of pink on the cherry tree – but the animals that had gathered by the back fence behind it were looking in a different direction.

Once he'd shifted his head into line with their own, John's gaze soon settled on a greyish patch of sky above what could be seen of the brooding waters of Loch Eye, and there he had the mirror he'd been looking for. So it would no doubt have been several minutes he stood there, watching what was due to happen later on that day, before he pulled the tweed bonnet back into its proper place, with the brim at a slight tilt to the line of his forehead, and slowly walked back into the house.

Anyone would think that a rare commotion such as John had witnessed could hardly be forgotten again just like that – unless it was his memory starting to go. But according to himself, that's more often than not been the way of it with the second sight, ever since it was granted to him, and that's going back almost fifty years to a young loon in his twenties. All he was left with then, sitting in the kitchen over a cup of tea and his pipe, was a certain tiredness that slowly drifted away along with the last of the smoke from the briar.

Meanwhile, the planes would have started their dive-bombing practice over the Mhorrich, a few miles to the north, sending the thunder of scorched air echoing round the whole peninsula, but John was as used to it by now as anyone else in the area. In fact, the background noise was normal enough for him to pay it little heed when he got up again to fill the bucket with warm water, drop a sponge in it, and jam a folded newspaper in his pocket.

One by one he cleaned all the top windows until there was only the one with the gull's mess on it left to do. By then the planes would have been away again, back off to Lossiemouth more than likely, or else to Kinloss, and in the long silence they left behind them John began to feel someone standing at the foot of the ladders.

'Mr MacKenzie?'

'Aye.' John didn't need to turn his head round to know he'd taken an instant dislike to the man waiting on him down below, stranger though the man was. But he kept himself civil. 'I'll be with you directly.' He finished wiping the glass dry with the last ball of newspaper, while a single reconnaissance plane, out to take photos of the practice target, sent a distant boom through the air and was gone again. And right enough, by the time he'd climbed back down the steps with the bucket, he was in fact more than civil. 'I think they have learned their technique from the aeroplanes.' He started washing out the dirty sponge with a slow humour.

The stranger looked puzzled. Then the penny dropped: 'Ah, you mean the seagulls.'

With a vague nod of the head, John went around picking up

the wet gobs of paper he'd dropped on the path, hardly surprised to find his visitor looking much the way he'd pictured him. The dark blue cord trousers and the matching waterproof anorak were just the sort of neutral clothes the man would choose to make his appearance in, for he would be a sceptic, bent on testing John's powers by giving him no outward clue to his identity.

On that score, however, the stranger had been less than successful. Aye, the clothes fitted the man well enough, yet the man did not altogether fit the clothes: he would look more at home in his city suit. That would make far more sense of the close-cropped brown hair and the beard – a professional beard if ever John had set eyes on one. And the receding hairline, with the odd fleck of grey in it, would probably place the stranger in his early forties, more or less what he'd reckoned when he first heard the voice. All that aside though, it was the narrow blue eyes, and what more than likely lay behind them, that kept John in mind of his first feelings about the man. 'And you'll be?'

'Richard.' The man had a certain strength in his own grip too, though it would never be a match for John's, even if he ever lived that long. 'Richard Britten.'

'You'll come inside, Mr Britten.' John led the way with the bucket, emptying it in the sink and putting it by before he filled the kettle. The man's hand had been slightly damp to the touch, but it was hardly unusual for people to be a bit on edge when they came to visit. There would even be some secret part of the sceptical Richard Britten that believed there was really something in it – the second sight, that is to say. Otherwise he would hardly have made the journey. 'You've not come by the road.' John had noticed that the polished shoes and the cuffs of the cord trousers had fresh mud on them.

'No, I took a farm track and then walked round by the lake – the lock, rather.'

John nodded 'Loch Eye.'

'It's very scenic.'

John fetched two cups and saucers out of the cupboard. 'In its season…'

Now he'd been invited into the house, the stranger was even more eager to make a good impression, and that was normal enough too. Folk always seemed to think that their personal manner would affect what John saw in the future, as if that had ever made a blind jot of difference: now there was *real* superstition for you. 'I found a very restful spot by the water.' Richard was still trying to be pleasant while John filled the pot. 'Before the planes arrived, at any rate. Practicing, presumably?'

'Aye. They have a target out there on the Mhorrich, on the far side of the loch.' John fitted the lid on the pot and covered it with the knitted cosy. Then, for the first time, pity got the better of his dislike for Richard Britten when he looked directly into the narrow blue eyes and saw the closeness of the man's death. 'Thon spot by the water,' John found himself asking, though he wasn't sure why: 'would you be able to point it out to me?'

The man donned his puzzled look again, but he followed John back out the door and down to the garden gate where he duly pointed east. 'Over that way. A little further to the right, I think. Just beyond that clump of trees.'

'And would you say you felt at home there?'

'I don't quite understand …'

'It's a simple question, mun. Would you say you felt at home there?'

'Well – yes.' Richard's politeness was becoming strained. 'What on earth is so important about the place?'

John slowly shook his head. 'I'm trying to mind.' He scanned the landscape, but it wouldn't come back to him. And when the next wave of planes broke the silence, he was still standing there and still it wouldn't come back to him. 'I must beg your pardon, Mr Britten.' He put a sympathetic hand on his visitor's shoulder. 'We'd best go in and have our tea before it gets cold.'

The stranger's eye, on the lookout by now for some explanation for the old man's odd behaviour, would no doubt conclude in passing that he was a widower, watching him pour out the tea. And that would certainly be correct so far as it went. But an eye with a longer experience of John would be aware that his awkwardness in doing women's work around the house was a consequence of trying to do it someone else's way, and that trying to do it someone else's way was John's own quiet way of keeping the memory of his wife alive. 'Will you have a biscuit with it, Mr Britten?' He'd be slowly working free the round top on the tin, the way that Mrs MacKenzie used to do.

'I'll have a cigarette instead, if you don't mind.'

'Aye, mun. Have your smoke by all means.' John pressed the airtight lid closed again and tapped out the pipe in the metal pocket he'd made to fit below the Rayburn door. 'I'll join you myself in a minute.' He rested the briar back in the ashtray and loosened the pulley rope.

Richard Britten had noticed the things hanging from a bar of the pulley on their separate bits of string: about half a dozen of them, the size and shape of black puddings wrapped in dirty looking bandages. And now he was to find out what they were. Once John had untied one from the centre rung where it had been drying out over the winter, and cut the tight cotton bindings open, there it was: a long lump of tobacco, solid as a half pound of Walnut Plug, and dark as the rum that had soaked through the cured leaves from last year's plants. Richard voiced a polite interest in the proceedings: 'I wouldn't have thought you could grow tobacco this far north.'

'There's many a thing can be done if you have a mind to.' John would be cutting off a small pile of flakes with the penknife, then rubbing it up between his thumb and forefinger.

'You have a greenhouse, then?'

'No. This is out the garden.' John filled the pipe and tamped it down with the blackened matchbox after he put a light to it. 'It's a guy coarse smoke, mind you.' The humour was back in his eye, with the blue smoke filling the room like the waves of the sea. 'And now, Mr Britten, is there something I can do for you?'

As far as Richard was concerned, things weren't going quite according to plan. The way he'd seen it beforehand, he'd pay whatever price – within reason – was demanded for the consultation, and then leave – either enlightened, or (far more likely) duped by a charlatan. But such was his faith in the power of money, it had never crossed his mind until now that his request might actually be refused. Under the circumstances, a direct and businesslike approach seemed to be the best ploy. 'I'd like to pay you for a consultation. I've been told you can see into the future.'

'And who would be telling you that?' John can be as fly as a fox when the mood takes him.

'A friend.' Richard decided to come right out with it and name the person. Time was marching on after all. 'You told him he'd go to the States and be very successful. You were absolutely right.'

'I don't mind on that part of it,' John puffed away on the pipe. 'I mind the man himself, though. A great love of geology in him. Off he had us on an outing to Hugh Miller's cottage over there on the Black Isle, and then it was down to Rockfield for a look at the raised beach –'

'I'm afraid you have mixed him up with someone else. My friend's a physicist.'

'A physicist, aye.' John frowned. 'For his living. But were you not telling me he's a friend of yours? You seem to know remarkably little about the man.'

'Perhaps I should have said an acquaintance – a former colleague.'

'Aye, perhaps.' The frown was on John's face still. Then he was quiet a while, staring off into space. 'And perhaps you'll be pleased to know your acquaintance is in good spirits in his new home across the water.'

It was the first time a smile had crossed the stranger's face, even if it was a smile of pure derision. 'Are you trying to tell me –'

'I think, Mr Britten –' John was scarcely able to hide his annoyance with the man '– that I would be ill-advised to tell you anything beyond what mainly interests you: yourself. And to that end you will perhaps be kind enough to lend me the green fountain pen that you keep in your inside pocket.'

'How the devil –'

'I have no truck with the devil, Mr Britten.' John could see he'd given the stranger a fair turn there. 'If you wish me to tell you what I see, you will simply lend me the pen.'

Out of the inside pocket of the anorak came the pen anyway, and John sat holding it in his free hand a long time, until the pipe was done. From what the stranger had to say for himself afterwards, the old man's eyes seemed to be looking through him and past him at the same time, and the cat had got his tongue again, with not a single word coming out of him.

It was his sense of smell, though, that John was paying heed to while he had the pen in his hand. First of all, the vague scent of linoleum polish came off it, putting him in mind of the long, soulless corridors he could see his visitor walking through. Then came the rank smell of the man's ruthless ambition and, right enough, John could see him finally ensconced in the office he coveted so much. Yet for all the outward similarity of features, the man in the grand office was no longer recognisable as the same man that sat before him, and once again John could see how near his visitor was to his death.

It took a while longer before he tried to put it into plain words that the stranger might understand. 'You are a man of science, Mr Britten. That will hardly be news to you.' John gave him back the pen at last. 'And if your science has brought fear into the world along with its many marvels, you consider that is no concern of yours. For you are a man near-consumed by ambition, and I do not speak of ambition for the world, Mr Britten – that it might be a better place for folks to live in – but with ambition of the narrowest kind that sees no more in a person than his usefulness to you. Or the lack of it. Aye, mun: small wonder you want to know what the future holds so you can take a rest from your perpetual scheming –'

'I –'

'Hear me out, Richard Britten.' John went on with hardly a pause. 'You have not come here to converse with me about modern physics, and so much the better for that, no doubt. If you cannot even believe your own science when it tells you there is more than one future, you will easily discredit anything John MacKenzie has to say. But I say to you now that a man with the very likeness of you, down to the last hair in his beard, will indeed become the head of your department.'

John watched the brief spark of pleasure flash in the blue eyes. It was as if he'd finally struck the flint behind them. 'And I must tell you also that a man with the very likeness of one that sits before me, a mean-spirited man whose word has rarely been worth the breath it took to utter, will die this same day.'

It's hard to say exactly how long the two of them would have sat there looking at each other, with Richard feeling all of a sudden as tired as John must have done. And though they both recall it

being a long silence, there would surely have been the occasional
cackling of the geese and the hens outside the window as well as
the drone of the planes coming in from the north, even if neither
of them had an ear for it.

Anyway, it was Richard Britten who made the first move, when he
looked at his watch and it came as some surprise to him to find it
was that late on. 'Goodbye, Mr MacKenzie,' said he, back to his old
polite self again seemingly, and telling John that he had his lunch
booked at the Fearn hotel. But what still passed for politeness was
now little more than a curb on his anger.

'And will you be going back to your hotel by the same way you
came, Mr Britten?'

The truth of the matter was that Richard had an overwhelming
urge to get out of the old man's company with no further ado and
back down to the banks of Loch Eye where he'd stopped on his way
to visit the seer. He was still quite shaken by what John had had to
say, and he needed somewhere safe where he could have a private
think to himself. In fact, he was already on his way to the door. 'It
would be quicker than walking round by the main road.'

'It would that.' John got up out his own chair. But though he
still couldn't mind on why, he knew that he had to keep the stranger
from leaving yet. 'You might recall that the matter of payment was
mentioned.'

That stopped Richard right enough, if not for long by the looks
of it. Taking his hand off the door, he pulled the wallet out his hip
pocket with a speed that put John in mind of someone drawing a
pistol. 'And exactly how much do you consider I owe you for the
privilege of listening to all that mumbo-jumbo, not to mention
your downright rudeness?'

'If there's money burning that much of a hole in your pocket,
there are those more in need of it than myself.' John had the frown
back on his face, even if he kept his voice as meek as a lamb's. 'I
have another small job to do yet the day, and I'd appreciate your
assistance with it.'

'I prefer to pay you in cash, Mr. MacKenzie.' Richard was
fingering the notes impatiently. 'I've already told you I don't want
to be late for lunch, and I have to drive back down south this

afternoon.'

But John was thrawn. 'I believe it was yourself that first made any mention of payment. And I had taken you for a man of your word.'

It was a difficult decision for the stranger to make, particularly when he didn't realise that his life depended on it. He'd hardly developed any great liking for the seer, and he'd even calculated that with no phone in the house, nor any cottages within shouting distance, there was little that John could do to stop him leaving, with or without making payment of any kind. So, to this day, Richard Britten still doesn't know what made him decide to stay. He gave way in the end, still hoping he'd have a little time left to stop by the loch before getting back to the hotel. 'Provided it doesn't take too long.'

'We will be as quick as we can.' John slowly led the way back outside, where the ladders were still propped up against the front wall.

'Would you be kind enough to take them down and bring them to the garage, Mr Britten?' John went on ahead to open the wooden door of the outhouse that was built on to the gable. Once it would have been a garage, right enough, but John now evidently used it as a workshop – and, from the looks and the smell of it, for a stable and a henhouse as well. 'It's a case of replacing the broken pane in thon skylight.' He showed Richard where the ladders should be placed inside the garage, with the top ends of the shafts wedged between two of the sloping rafters.

'I'd be much obliged if you could bring the whole window down for me.' John held the foot of the steps while his assistant went up them. 'As you'll see, Mr Britten, it's a metal casement and there will be a fair weight in it. If you open the window about ninety degrees, you should be able to slide it free of the hinge. Aye, that's the very dab, Mr Britten. Canny does it on the way down.' He was soon helping Richard with it on to the bench. 'I'm much obliged to you.'

'Right. You're very welcome, I'm sure. Goodbye, Mr MacKenzie.'

But John knew he still had to detain the man a while yet. 'I had been hoping that you'd also be kind enough to take the window back up the steps for me after I've put the new pane in.'

'And then that's it? I have your word on that?'

'Absolutely, Mr Britten. You've already been extremely generous with your time.' John began knocking the broken glass out the frame with the hammer, while Richard looked on impatiently. 'The job might go a little quicker if you could roll me out some fresh putty.' The seer pointed to the plastic tub that was sitting on the bench. Then he set about chipping the old, brittle stuff off the astragals and sweeping it away into the bin along with the fragments of glass.

By the time he got round to cleaning the rust off the metal frame with the wire brush, Richard hadn't so much as taken the top off the tub, for his fury at being manipulated by this crazy old man was reaching its peak. A powerful part of him was still dying to run out of the garage and down to that spot on the banks of Loch Eye before it was too late –

But too late for what?

Slowly and mysteriously, all Richard's anger vanished into thin air, and he found himself standing there content as a child, rolling out the lengths of putty and lining them up on the bench until John said there were enough. And indeed, Richard started to feel as content as a child to be helping the old man with the thick, snowy hair and the white moustache, lightly stained in amber above the lip from the smoking of his tobacco and the occasional drink of whisky. Working the tools that had seen him through most of a lifetime, John's body moved to such a simple, honest music – the firm scratch of the cutter marking the glass and the satisfied snap of a clean break – it was a music that Richard wanted to learn.

'If you will just have a little more patience with me, Mr Britten, I'll have it done in no time now.' John got on with the job while his visitor wandered off through some straw to the back door in the garage and looked out on the small piece of land where a few hens, two geese, a goat and an old pony made up an odd assortment of beasts. 'They were not wanted – except for the hens of course.' John didn't look up from his work of placing the pane in the soft putty and cleaning off the surplus with the chisel. 'They come in now and again when the weather gets dreich.' He turned the frame over and pressed in more of the strips that Richard had rolled, setting the chisel at a steady angle to finish off the job.

'It's too late now.'

'Too late for what, Mr Britten?'

'Was I talking out loud? I don't know. I really don't know.'

'I'm awful sorry, mun. I can't mind either.' John could feel a genuine affection for the stranger now in all his confusion, for it was a confusion that John himself shared. 'That's the animals late for their lunch as well as ourselves.' He made light of it while his visitor carried the heavy window back up the ladder, trying not to get his hands in the wet putty before it was back in place.

All Richard's hurry to be gone had disappeared along with his anger, and after he was down again, he folded up the steps and parked them neatly on the garage floor before he followed John out. 'All the windows cleaned and repaired, Mr MacKenzie,' he heard himself saying, 'and still we see through a glass darkly...'

'You might well put it that way, Mr Britten.' John closed the garage door behind them. 'But I do appreciate your assistance, and I need detain you no longer.'

Richard smiled a wry smile. 'To be perfectly honest, I have to admit you've given me quite a lot to think about.' He was still reluctant to be off, but John seemed not to have heard him as he led the way down to the garden gate, then turned around to wait on him.

By that time Richard had almost got used to the noise of the planes himself, even if the latest roar sounded closer than any so far and his inner ear told him there was also something very different about it. What he actually noticed first of all, though, was the same expression gathering on the seer's face that he'd had not so long ago when he asked for the fountain pen. It all seemed to focus on the widening nostrils as he stood there watching the huddle of animals at the fence behind the cherry tree. Then his head began nodding slowly up and down as he turned in the same direction they were looking and gazed into the murky eastern sky. 'I mind now.' He seemed to be talking only to himself. 'I mind now, all right –'

'*That plane's going to crash.*'

'Aye, Mr Britten. Observe where it comes down.'

Above Loch Eye, the bright unfolding of parachutes caught

Richard's eye a moment before his last glimpse of the plane, which was heading for the very spot where he might so easily have been sitting. Then came an end to the painful whine of the engines in an explosion that set the whole of Fearn village shaking.

THE CRASH

The Crash

Building the oil rigs up here was going to bring prosperity to the area and stop us youngsters drifting south – so they said. There was a certain truth in it, too: at least to begin with. When the whole business started up, school-leavers our age could be full-time welders after a six week course in the old Tain Academy, and be walking out the site gates at Nigg on a Thursday with good money in our pockets.

What they called the industrial gypsies – the men that had been camping down at Nigg to lay the foundations for the dry dock – were already back off on their travels by then. So if the likes of us had been stopped from drifting off with them, we were either working on the site itself or on the new housing schemes and the bungalows for the next wave of incomers from the south. Some of them turned out to be industrial gypsies too, in their own way, but there were others came to like the place and the people well enough to stay on, feast or famine. Alec was one of them.

He kept himself pretty much to himself at first, always eating his piece outside on his own if it was half-decent weather. Anywhere at all on the site he'd park himself, as long as he could look out west across the firth at the place he was renting near the Invergordon harbour. We'd see him when we came back out the canteen, safety helmet still on, finishing off the flask of coffee. And the cigarette pointing straight up in the air with smoke drifting out the top, for all the world like it was mimicking the chimney of the aluminium smelter over the water. At the end of the day, it was 'Cheers,' and off he'd go in the red van that had *ALEC* written up in big letters on the windscreen – the same thing that the rest of us used to do, whatever kind of machine we had on the road at the time.

That's the high priority in these parts: wheels. There used to be three of us would fill up the tank and pile into an old Ford after work on a Thursday to see what talent there was in the area. But one night, all we picked up was Alec. Down by the Invergordon docks he was, sitting on a capstan looking out on the firth, the same as he did at work. Except, of course, he was looking the opposite way, over at the Nigg shore where the back shift would still be working

17

on Highland One – nearly half-finished it would have been – under the floodlights. There was nothing else for it but to take him off for a pint: he seemed that down in the dumps.

'Cheers.' He was never much of a drinker in those days, Alec, so it didn't take much to loosen his tongue: the wife had walked out on him. People up here were too clannish the way she saw it, and she couldn't stand the isolation any longer. Another pint, and he was telling us how he always believed marriage would be a case of living for the other person, like they said in the vows, but it didn't seem to be working out that way. Maybe she was right, he couldn't help wondering, and they should never have moved up here where they hardly knew a soul. But then there was his work to consider too. What a state to be in: he didn't know if he was coming or going. To cut a long story short, the teenage bride Alec showed us in a photograph had taken the train back to Glasgow, and either he followed her in the red van or it was divorce.

Straightforward enough.

But *clannish? Us?* We were really peeved. 'Stay on, Alec,' we said. 'We're your mates.' And we promised him a party on the Saturday to prove it. It was going to be his twenty-first birthday, after all.

That's when he met Shona. If it wasn't for wanting to make him feel more at home here, we could have seen him far enough: Shona's still a fine catch for any man. But none of us had ever been able to get a move with her and, right enough, the two of them seemed to be made for each other.

What a change came over Alec. Maybe Shona started spending the weekends ironing out the creases on his forehead one by one, and putting the smile back on his face for the Monday morning, because he was soon looking younger than the first day he walked through the Nigg gates. A lot more sociable too, laying off in the canteen to all and sundry about union policy, and what the government – still Labour it was, in power – should be doing if it really wanted to improve the country. Not that we paid any heed to his patter. We used to laugh it off: 'As red as his van, Alec.'

Conditions were still good down at the site, all things considered, and when Highland One was launched there was genuine pride in it from top management right down to the blokes that swept up the floors. Some sight it was, too, the launching. The press and the TV cameras were all over the place that day, with ordinary people out in their hundreds as well for view of the platform up on its end at last, all ready to be towed out into the firth. Alec had filled up the van with a gang of us from work – girlfriends and wives included – and for all his smart talk it has to be said in his favour that he was as chuffed as any of us, standing there on the jetty with his arm round Shona, watching the rig float out between the Sutors and then off to the Forties Field.

His divorce had come through about a month before, but if he hadn't been celebrating that in the usual style, he was hardly planning on getting drunk just because the first platform had left our yard without sinking. So that was certainly another thing to be said in his favour – at least compared with the rest of us in those days, what with our celebration ceilidh all arranged for the evening. And with Alec happy enough to stay on the wagon for such occasions, we soon got into the habit of taking a lift with him there and back to other local dances and the like. Maybe we were starting to get some sense. Most of us had been settling down a bit – wife, kids, TV – and there didn't seem much point in ending up disqualified after an evening on the bevy. Or piling the motor up.

But even after we stopped gunning down the roads ourselves, there would still be some wild drivers about any night of the week. 'Kamikaze Highlanders.' That's how Alec would laugh them off when he wasn't at the wheel. On the way back home, though, there was bound to be more than one pair of undipped headlights swerving round a blind corner, forcing him to crash down to third and hug the van to his own side of the road. That would wipe the smile off his face. 'Bloody eejits,' he called them then.

We could see his point of view. Alec wasn't the only one that had finally come to the conclusion that he had more than himself to live for.

The only time we'd see him driving on his own any more would be up and down the Nigg road to work, and even then he never seemed quite alone, with *SHONA* written up on the passenger side of the windscreen. The rest of the time she'd be there in person, giving us a big wave when they passed. Or else we'd see the empty van parked, down in Balintore say, on a Saturday, and they'd be off walking over the Nigg Hill, or out along the beach to the cliffs, holding hands like they were still in their teens. Or if we saw the red van sitting over the wall from the manse in Portmahomack on a good summer's afternoon, we'd pull in beside it and the kids would soon find the two of them sunbathing in the dunes. Always a good word for the kids they'd have, and always a little something for them at Christmas too, although we were never done telling them they shouldn't go to the bother.

When the two of them moved into one of those modernised farm cottages up the Edderton hill, it was the kids as much as anyone that would egg us on to take a spin up there on a Sunday. Alec would take them swimming in the pool under the waterfall in the good weather, and Shona would be forever giving them biscuits and orange juice and the like. What a view of the Sutherland coast they had out the north windows too, with the sea and the straths and the woods changing colour all the time. Shona would make up some cock-and-bull story about the long hill that you can see on the skyline – the one they call the Crouching Lion – and the next thing Alec would be telling the little ones it wasn't a lion at all, but an old grey whale stranded up there, and they'd be laughing again when he told them how it all came about.

Soon they had the garden out behind the cottage looking like a little Eden, and they looked set to live out the rest of their days there. The only thing we were waiting on was for Alec to take the next step. Once bitten, twice shy, we reckoned – he'd come round to it in the end. But it was taking him a while. 'Time you tied the knot,' we used to tell him.

Married or not, though, the honeymoon was over down at the site with the men being laid off and taken back on again depending on whether there were new orders coming in, and Alec was getting more involved with his union work. Not that it kept him in steady employment any more than the rest of us. A union can't create jobs – except maybe in the union itself, and Alec was never that far in with them.

With Shona working in the hairdresser's down in Tain and the two of them living together, he couldn't get Benefit when he was out of work, so they had to get by one way or another on Shona's wages and any work that Alec could pick up with the van. He'd do small removals then, as well as the regular roadie work that he did for a local band whether he was working at Nigg or not. And there was the spell when he did the collections from Inverness for a fruit and vegetable retailer, but when the work picked up again at the site he had to give that up. It all kept the van on the road anyway, so he could drive Shona in to her own work and collect her at the end of the day.

The next thing we knew, the TV was telling us it was a winter of discontent, and we had to agree with a lot of what they were saying. Not Alec, though. With the election coming up in the spring, he was out canvassing for Labour, and he took a lot of stick from us for that. 'We thought you were *against* the government, Alec.' We used to try and wind him up, but he could see the funny side of it himself.

'Poacher turned gamekeeper.' He'd grin, and carry on slapping his stickers on helmets and jackets and anything else that moved.

'You're wasting your time, Alec,' we told him. 'There's never been a Labour man elected here yet, and there never will be'

'There's a first time for everything.' He tried to keep his end up, but he wasn't daft. He knew as well as anyone else that it was a token gesture.

After the government changed he was back at his union work, even addressing the meetings now and again, small as they were. By that time, of course, hardly anyone wanted to spend a minute longer than they had to out there, so it was in the canteen that we'd pick up most of his patter about the change in management style – as if we needed telling. Respect for the working man was a thing of the past. But at least there was still some work available, even if there was no telling how long it would last.

Before he knew it, Alec had been here well over ten years – the place had got that much of a grip on him – and he was long since part of the local scenery to us.

They say that Shona thought it was high time she had a husband and a baby, and that Alec still wasn't having any of it, but we'd never hear anything about it from themselves directly. No doubt there was some truth in the rumour they were going through a bad patch though, with the two of them cancelling their holiday to Spain at the last minute, and Shona off to Edinburgh instead all of a sudden. The next thing, Alec was off after her in the van, but we were too busy trying to get away ourselves to take much of it in at the time.

He was all on his own in the Edderton cottage when we got back, with hardly a word to say to anyone, so we arranged to take him out for a quiet pint to mark his birthday before we went back to Nigg, thinking that might loosen his tongue a bit. As things turned out, it was the first time we ever saw him in his cups, pouring doubles and chasers down all night, but even then there wasn't a single word about Shona crossed his lips. It was the first time we saw him lose the rag too, that night. Some Invergordon bloke that had lost his job when the aluminium smelter closed was laying off about the incomers, and we could see that Alec was taking it all in at the same time we were talking to him. 'And where d'yous think Glasgow people come from in the first place?' He was up off his pew like a shot before anyone could grab him, with both the bloke's jacket lapels in his fists.

'Calm down, Alec.' At least we caught up with him in time to stop the head going in, and the next thing he was all apologies, ordering drinks all round, starting with the Invergordon man. That calmed things down a bit. Then, before anyone else could get a word in edgeways, he was off on a long ramble about his family history. Back three, four generations of working men he went, back to Daniel MacLean's father being evicted from the croft – but he didn't remember a thing about it the following day.

Maybe that's because Shona turned up again, as suddenly as she'd disappeared.

And it was easy enough forgotten compared with the battle that was brewing up at the site when we went back. *The Orange Juice Strike*, the big newspapers and the media were soon calling it, and for once Alec wasn't the only one that was furious. A lot the welders cared, whether it was free Company orange juice or public water they were getting to stop the dehydration, in that oven they were working in, as long as they could get out for a breather to drink it.

But the scaffolding had all been dismantled while we were away on holiday – that's why the rest of us had to come out in support.

What a shambles. It was letters from the management one day dismissing the lot of us, and union meetings in Tain the next with the London leaders up addressing us, and Alec right in there trying to sell us his left wing papers again on the way out. Then another letter calling us back to work, so the next we saw of Alec was on the picket line at the Nigg gates. The local bobbies even had to be called out that day to stop some of us doing each other in, but eventually it was all sorted out, and back we went to finish the contract and pick up our redundancy notices.

When Alec said he was finished with the whole business, we took it with a pinch of salt at first. We'd said the same thing ourselves many a time, then back we went at the first opportunity. What else could we do? The kids were all settled in at school with their exams coming up, and what other work was there up here for the likes of us that would pay as well? Not that the opportunity came for nearly a year after the strike, and even then it was a smallish contract that would hardly require twelve hundred men. But Alec didn't bat an eyelid when the news came through. He was staying out.

Of course, we hadn't been seeing as much of the two of them as we used to. For one thing, the little ones weren't so little any more, coming up to an age where they would rather be lying in the bath in their jeans, shrinking them down to size, than out swimming under the waterfall. And, for another thing, Alec's van was off the road. It would still go all right, but the bodywork was getting a bit rusted by then and it would never have passed its MOT. One of the garage boys that played in the band always used to let Alec use the ramp when things were quiet and do the work himself, but this time he hadn't bothered. The garden was going to rack and ruin too.

It seemed that the only thing he did bother doing any more was taking long walks and hauling any firewood he came across back home with him to the cottage. That and the drinking, of course. We could see now why he never used to touch it as a rule, and it was hard to know if it was better to visit him or not with the whisky brought out as soon as anyone arrived. One or two of us that were in work at the time tried to give him a sub to get the van back on the road, thinking that might bring him back into contact with people more. But he was thrawn: he could get the machine roadworthy off his own bat if he so desired. 'I've got savings,' he said, although they could hardly have totted up to much by then with a bottle always on the go.

He'd be pleased as a puppy to see us any time we called by, but as time went on it was becoming harder and harder to talk to him. 'What have you been doing with yourself then, Alec?' we'd say, and there was only ever the one answer.

'Collecting dead wood.' He'd look fair chuffed with himself, pointing to the great piles of it outside the window where he used to have the garden lovely.

Then he'd be offering us a dram again. 'Save it for yourself, Alec.' We could hardly go drinking the man's whisky when there was no telling where the money was coming from.

In the end he'd hardly ever get off his chair, according to Shona. 'There's almost enough dead wood collected now,' he'd say, sitting there with the glass in his hand, looking out of the window. 'And then there's going to be a big blaze.'

'Well, you take care of yourself, Alec –'

'Enough to burn the whole house down.'

He wouldn't even notice us slipping off into the kitchen for a word with Shona, because it was her we were worried about as well. It was on Shona's forehead that the creases were now, and Alec not even fit to do his own ironing, far less anyone else's.

'He's surely not thinking about setting the place on fire?'

'No, no. That's not what he's meaning. He'll get over it.' She would try and put a brave face on it all. But it wasn't much of a life for her any more, walking all that way down to the main road for a bus in to work in all weather, and back again to Alec in a state like that.

It couldn't go on forever.

There was one night Shona decided to take a drink along with him to see if that would help them sort things out, and they'd perished more than a bottle between them before Alec got up out the chair all of a sudden and into the red van. She could hear that he was heading up the hill, and after that he would have turned south, because it was a few miles further down the Struie road that the van was found early the following morning.

Whether it was black ice on the road, or mechanical failure, or Alec swerving to avoid some 'bloody eejit' – or Alec turned into a Kamikaze Highlander himself that night – was never altogether established. All we know for certain is that the van must have been going at a fair lick before it left the road. Then it would have turned over two or three times before it hit the boulder that smashed the windscreen to smithereens and killed him outright.

There was no big explosion, or even a fire like there would have been on the TV, and now and again it's hard to wake up to the fact that there's so little drama for the likes of us that are living on. All the drama's on the television now. Shona says she watches a lot of it since she went to stay with her mother over there in Lochinver.

We all do these days.

Watch enough of it of course, and there's always some new slant on things. There was a bloke on not long ago with a shaven head and a brown robe, saying unemployment is a great chance for people to discover themselves and reject this materialistic society we live in. Well, at least that made some change from being either pitied or condemned, because it's hard to say which is the worse.

And, right enough, that's maybe what we should be telling the TV licence people next time it's due, and the Council when they want the rent. Or the wife when she's going crackers with us getting in the way of the housework. And maybe that's what to tell the kids when their hearts are all set on a new bike for Christmas. And, if that doesn't work, we can always say that drifting south is the best thing to do when the school's over.

That's where the work is these days – so they say.

Or maybe things will pick up again at Nigg.

But it's not that easy to exist on maybes. We've been idle a long time now since that last order was finished, with hardly a hundred men employed on basic maintenance out at the site these days. And there were few enough of the five thousand men that once worked at Nigg ever got on to the television, so we're hardly expecting a repeat. Set up the cameras on the Invergordon shore after dark, and right enough the place is still lit up like a London

25

bank with walls of solid gold.
      But it's empty as a grave inside.

A LAMENT FOR THE UNION

A Lament For The Union

S he used to hear a distant pibroch sound on the breeze those autumn evenings, back in that year when the child was still newly formed inside her. And when her husband was away at sea, she'd often climb the low summit of the hill and sit awhile, listening to that sad and lonely music, even if it was no more than some trick of the wind.

After darkness had returned to the land, only Inverness, tinsel-lit, would remain in view to remind her that she lived in the lengthening shadow of the twentieth century. Strings of white and orange lights would glint like electric dewdrops on an unseen web suspended between the gentle inland slopes and the foreshore, where two last shimmering tentacles of light, separated by the invisible Ness, snaked into the blackness of the firth. Invisible also was the hospital which required her to make such frequent visits. But to the west she could clearly see the single beacon of light that marked entry to the Caledonian Canal while, to the east, temporary floodlights played on the foundations of the bridge that would eventually link the Highland capital to their side of the water.

The completion of the bridge would cut her husband's travelling time back and forth to Aberdeen, the main base for his off-shore assignments, and he was all in favour of that. But for her own part, she would miss her solitary walks into North Kessock, timed to allow her an unhurried cup of tea before the arrival of the ferryboat from Inverness. And she would miss that brief sea journey across the narrow neck of firth, inhaling the salt breeze before she made her way through the traffic fumes of the town to the hospital.

Strange how her first recollections from that period were always of the times she'd spent alone. For in the deep quiet of her being her husband had been ever present, whether at his work of inspecting the platforms or at home with her, forever finding new jobs that needed doing round the house before the baby arrived. Even those memorable trips across the water on her own had been very much the exception. Far more often they'd visited the hospital together, and it was together they'd driven the long road round by

Beauly the day the consultant decided to break the news to them. They said yes, they would like to see the x-rays for themselves, and yes, they would let him know their decision by the end of the week. And yes, oh yes, there had only been one decision possible, for what kind of life could such a creature ever have had?

And so it was a sad Christmas that year, leaving her still weak as a kitten after the operation. There were complications, so they'd been told before she left the hospital, and they'd been strongly advised not to try again.

Though her husband seemed swift to embrace the sorrow as if it was some forgotten friend from long ago, it constantly stood across her own path that winter like some malevolent stranger whose challenge she was not yet strong enough to meet. No longer could she summon up the energy to climb the hill, and only once did she hear the phantom music trudge slowly towards the house before it got lost in the silence of the drifting snow ...

It was a hard winter. No matter how much coal she heaped on the fire, even with the central heating fully on as well, she never felt warm except when her husband was with her. When he was away the days and nights seemed unending, and the cold seemed to be permanently lodged inside her. The new fear of abandonment which had swept over her heightened her normal fear for his safety at sea, and all she could do in his absence was to repeat to herself his time-worn reassurances. He was a Safety Officer after all, was he not? Ah, but finally the day came when she persisted too far in her concern and he said yes, of course, there were countless factors beyond his personal control. And in such an event there would be compensation –

Compensation? As if all the riches in the world could ever compensate her –

He'd become angry at that, instead of touched by her expression of dependence. No doubt he'd instinctively sensed that the right time had come to tell her to pull herself together, because it was soon after that she began to do so. Towards the end of April when she was given a clean bill of health at her final check-up, an impulse to break with her usual routine took hold of her, and instead of returning directly home by the ferry she boarded a Nairn bus, travelling through the built-up slopes of Drummossie as far as the Cumberland Stone, where she was the only passenger to get off.

The bleakness of Culloden Moor that day, at the same time of year the battle had been fought, was at first repellent to her as she slowly tramped round the site, avoiding treacherous bogs whose sparse reeds and rushes offered little indication of their real depths. But in the end she began to feel a melancholy kinship with the place, for men also had had the life torn out of them there – by bayonet and by bullet.

And when she stopped by those mossy mounds where the heather has for two centuries and more refused to grow, she fancied she could hear low murmurings at that most mysterious place. The words were not words she could understand, but their resonant tones spoke eventually to her of some profound acceptance lodged deep within the earth itself. Then it was that resignation began to wrap itself around her like a plaid against the spring chill, and the real healing could begin.

Soon she became familiar with the old story of how the victors at Culloden had gone on to terrorise the land by fire, sword and starvation, and how territory which the mighty Roman empire once considered too costly to subdue was at last turned to profit by replacing men with sheep. But if the land had a sorrowful past, that only brought her closer to it. Less and less did she think of the place she originally came from as the Home Counties, and even her father's loud boast that his daughters had been brought up on the fringe of the stockbroker belt was not loud enough to carry this far north.

Yet neither did her husband's gentle tones entirely compensate her for the independence she had lost, and steadily she went about reclaiming it. By the time she had her certificate to teach north of the border and her driving licence, she used the new bridge more than he did, motoring daily into Inverness where she taught for some years at the academy until a post more suited to her style came up in Alness.

By then the Party stickers and slogans on her car proclaimed her new loyalties in no uncertain manner: the English Scottish Nationalist, people called her. But they called her that to her face, and with a genuine personal liking for her, however much of an idealist she might be. And if her husband's attitude towards her politics was much the same, it only confirmed her suspicion that it probably took an outsider to see the true state of the country these days, with independence driven so long ago from a reality into a dream. Idealist or no, she was perfectly clear now that her future struggle lay in helping to turn that old dream of nationhood back into modern fact.

No doubt her trip to London for her youngest sister's wedding could only confirm her new outlook. As always before, those slick young City men with their salaried increments, their shrewd investments and their declarations of a personal interest impressed her mainly with their ultimate shallowness. But for the first time she saw their greed as more than a purely personal quality: it was a positive danger to other people.

And, after returning north, her disquieting vision of the metropolis and of the transatlantic empire which it served, lingered on. It made sense not only of the holes in kids' clothes and the emptiness behind their eyes as they mooched about the streets, but also of the occasional phone calls her husband had been making from home in more recent times. Although it was the tone rather than the substance of his conversations that carried through the closed door, she could hear a suppressed anger underlying his normal firm politeness, and she became increasingly aware that one of the many factors beyond his personal control was the willingness of his superiors to act on his reports and recommendations.

Her continuing anxiety about his safety had long since ceased to be a hysterical one, and she even liked to imagine that it had become an altogether impersonal one: that she was concerned, just as her husband was, for the safety of all working men offshore. Yet when the platform went down in that grey summer month, and the first word of it reached her on the TV news, it was his own hazel eyes and each clear-cut line of his face that she saw as her heart took an uncontrollable lurch. Within minutes his parents were on the phone, for none of them knew which assignment he'd been on at the time, and no immediate word was available from Aberdeen. What a relief, then, that he at least had been spared, when he phoned later in the evening to say he'd been in a different sector at the time and he wasn't required in the disaster area. He'd be coming home the following day.

Continually she'd tried to persuade him to quit his offshore work, applying a steady firmness of intention to match his own, but even now he still refused to consider it. He'd be taking that job in the Gulf he'd been promised next year as planned, and somehow that seemed to bring it all to a head, for she would not be going with him, however much a dying part of her might want to. She had hardly achieved her present standing in the community overnight, and an absentee councillor was the last thing a place with such a history needed, she told him lightly. (For the receiving of so much ironic humour had also taught her in the end how to deliver it.)

Her last public appearance as his wife was at a local service for two of the men who had gone down with the platform. Her husband knew neither of them much more closely than she did herself, and as she stood there, finally her own woman, she realised how solitary each of them had become, long before they'd agreed on the formalities of separation. But because their destiny had been for so long a shared one, each must continue for some time yet to be the nearest the other had to an intimate friend.

Such paradoxical thoughts occasionally interrupted the words that were spoken that morning, heartfelt and sincere though those words were. But when the words were over, the piper, who had also been listening in silence behind them, took up his stance outside the church, and all at once what she had taken for some fanciful dream of long ago became a stark reality as she recognised the pibroch from a past that belonged not only to the piper, but to herself as well now.

And now, looking into his steady eye, she could see for the first time a reflection not only of the sadness itself, but of the stoicism it took to forge that sadness into a monument as plain and eloquent as the uncut headstones at Culloden. And so, when a decent silence had elapsed, she felt impelled to ask the piper for the name of the music. 'It is called,' he told her, 'The Lament For The Union.'

AUDITION

Audition

— Sure thing. Take a pew. Really enjoyed the set, by the way.

— Nah. Thanks all the same. I'm fine with this. Don't let the punters here get you down, that's just their crack. If they didn't like it they'd have given you a hard time.

— Yup, but it's quiet everywhere just now. Don't let the numbers phase you. You'll get paid okay. No problem. It was a good set, very professional. Don't take it personal, that's the worst thing you could do. Nobody puts their hands together here even if they think it's brilliant. And see Calum, the bar manager, he's lousy with his advertising. Just that tiddling little poster in the window, see it?

— Well he didn't even put that up till this afternoon. Hopeless. Nobody ever has a clue who'll be gigging here on a Friday, just that there's likely to be something live. Anyway, the whole scene's dead this time of year: don't have to tell you blokes that. Inverness you're from, is it?

— Thought that's what Calum said. Exactly the same last Friday, anyway. About half a dozen punters still here when we finished up, and four of them just here for the pool table.

— Me? Nah. Not since last Friday, anyway. I quit. Just out for a pint tonight and watch some other musos sweat it out for a change. Seriously though, what you do's spot on or I wouldn't still be here. Calum's twigged it's good too. I was speaking to him earlier.

— *My* band? Wouldn't have called it that, exactly. Just me tacked on to a husband and wife team. Never again. Good singer, the husband; plays acoustic/electric and does the drum programming. But it's one of those scenes where he doesn't get out the door unless

37

the wife's playing bass along with him. That was the crack.

— Me? Just filling in on electric and doubling up on the choruses for a bit of pocket money after they fired the last bloke. I knew the score. Can't complain. Reckoned it wouldn't run more than six months before it all blew up, and I was pretty close. Give or take a week or two.

— Nah, you wouldn't have heard the name. We didn't go far afield. Local stuff, mostly. Commercial in Balintore, The Bridge up in Bonar – that sort of circuit. Only did one in Inverness. Agents seem to have the place pretty much sown up, that what you find?

— Anyway, they were only going for direct bookings, cash in hand.

— Now you're embarrassing me. *Three To The Bar* it was called. I mean, how corny can you get? Always hated that for a name. No regrets on that one ending. No way.

— Well, you'd only be hearing my side of the story, but I'd say it was mostly down to the wife. Real stars-in-my-eyes type. I mean, operating at a very high fantasy level. TV or bust, even if you're playing *Postman Pat*. Personally I reckon it was just one gig too many at The Arms here, and not a soul asking for their autographs. Getting harder and harder to see it as the first step on the glittery ladder, know what I mean?

— Sure thing. I mean, I take us for realists, gentlemen. Anyway, the three of us are here about this time last Friday packing up the gear when she starts throwing a right stushie. Says they're going to replace me with a sequencer and it'll work out a lot cheaper. So I hung fire, waiting for the husband to tell her she was out of order, but no way. All you get is the big silence, the *my-wife-right-or-wrong* routine. Just packed my gear in the car and left them to it. Regretted it a bit the following day, right enough.

— Nah, not the music: the casho. Totally forgot about it. No use trying to hit them for it later: they'd have blown it on a taxi getting themselves home. I was doubling as roadie, part of the deal. But not never no more. Rather be sitting here listening to what you blokes are doing – much more my line of country. Loved that version of *Stars On The Water,* by the way. Big New Country fan, me. And those variations on the old *Wonderful Tonight* riff were spot on.

— Yup, I know. But just getting bored with a lick isn't the same as being able to play round it like that. You're really the business on that electric. Couldn't begin to do some of that stuff. Years behind you there. What's the name, by the way?

— Also know as Fast Freddie, by any chance?

— Amazing. I was bound to hear you sooner or later. There's a lot of musicians been telling me to listen out for you. Shake on it, Freddie. Great playing. And who's your quiet friend?

— Good to meet you, Shug. Really solid vocal, and that acoustic works very nice on the blues stuff. Was that a Robert Johnson number, the one you did in F?

— Really? Been meaning to catch up on Gary Moore. One of those names keeps cropping up in the guitar mags. Pin him down one of these days.

— Nah, sound balance was fine the way it was. Checked it out from here and down the bar end too. Vocals were right where they should be, and not too much reverb. Balance between the guitars works fine, and the drum machine was pretty much where I'd put it myself. Good old Alesis SR16, is it?

— Yup, thought I recognised some of the patterns. Great machine for firing off live. Mine, you just get a one-bar repeat on the presets, so you have to step-write the whole track to get anything decent out of it. Only one thing, really – and it's not a criticism. Just that I can hear a gap where the bass-line would be. I mean, the bass-drum patterns are sound. Just that the bass-drum's down there in the low hertz all on its own. Hate to mention the word, but if you got a sequencer instead of just the drum machine, you could write a bass-line in as well. Just to fill in the sound more.

— Oh, I see. Why did he quit, then?

— Ah. Didn't know Ardersier was up and going again. Yup, that's a bit hefty if you're on twelves and trying to toe the family line in between times. Don't think I could hack it either. Glad I'm a man of leisure at the moment.

— Sure. Any guitar player ought to be able to cover bass, that's what I always say. Mind you, some people definitely have more of a feel for it. Without mentioning any names.

— Hang fire. We're not talking Flea here. Don't do any of that fancy right hand slap stuff. Dead simple what I do: just the basics. Juggle the chord notes about mostly – and not even that a lot of the time. Steady roots and fives, save the third for a quick filler if I use it at all. Unless it's a blues or a rock thing. I'm fairly sussed on that.

— Well, if I came to think about it, there's maybe six numbers in your set I could play on straight away. And that blues in D, with the relative minor variation? Liked that. Used to plaster distort all over *Should I Stay Or Should I Go?* and it was in a different key, but I could sort it out for bass pretty quick. And that Springsteen cover, used to do a version of it with *Jokers Wild*, except I was on electric rhythm and back-up vocals in that set-up.

— Ha, *Jokers Wild*. Yup, that was a bit more like what I like to do.

— Well, cheers, Freddie. Coming from you that means something. But I reckon your mates must have heard us on a good night. It was always a bit hit or miss with that band. Don't worry, Shug. That's just Calum getting rid of the punters. No margin on a lock-in tonight. Band always gets one after time, though, no problem.

— Cheers then, Shug. Just a half for me. And you'd better tell Calum I'm with you blokes. Otherwise I'm out the door with the rest of them. Tell him I'm giving you a hand to load up. I'm just trying to think – what was that other Clapton number you covered? The country rocker?

— Right. Of course. Couldn't remember the name of it for the life of me. Used to program it about 190 BPM. Yours sounds about the same, really kicking along. Best thing to do is just underline the guitar riff on the bass. Should be sound.

— Yup. Every band should have at least one Sally song. Surprised you don't cover any *Oasis,* by the way. Unless I missed it.

— Cheers, Shug. Freddie's just been telling me everything you don't like about *Oasis.*

— But you have to admit it goes down well with the punters. You get paid all right, by the way?

— Yup, he can be a bit dour, Calum, but I've never had any hassle with him on that front. Only thing that really gets to him is bands playing too loud. Never has them back. No second chances, nothing. Has he been filling in the diary, then?

— Great stuff. See, I told you. He'll let it ride this time of year so he's got steady bands when it picks up in the summer. Don't take a gig in The Caley, by the way, if you're playing here. You're either a Caley band or you're an Arms band – know what I mean? Too small a place, this. Anyway, if you blokes are serious, how about me coming along to a rehearsal and you can check me out?

— Come on. You're joking. I only know a bit more than half your second set, and I haven't heard your first set at all. Mind I came in when you were playing that *Del Amitri* cover? Can't remember

41

what it's called, but it's tricky. I'd need to work on that.

— You serious? You really want to chance it?

— Come on. That's real muso territory, The Market Bar. Don't want to screw up there.

— Well, you're the boss. If you really want to go for it. Got a spare list of what else you do?

— Jot down the keys as well, then, would you? Great. Bass guitar, bass amp. I've got a mate I can borrow them off. Anything else I need?

— Mike and stand, no problem. But I'd be better sorting out the bass-lines before I go for any harmonies. We're not talking Sting here, either. Better warn you. One step at a time.

— Well, yup. Probably could on a few of them straight away. Fair enough, we'll check it out. That's Calum getting restless back there, by the way. Time to shift the gear.

— Yup, on our way Calum. I'm just giving the boys here a hand. Great duo, eh?

— Always said you had good taste, Calum. Might be a trio next time they come back. Be seeing you.

WILDLIFE
FREEDOM

Wildlife Freedom

If long experience had left Ian better prepared than the others for a daily drenching – or for working a seven-day week, if it came to that – it had also warned him that his new recruits from the city might well hitch back there unless he gave them all some time out. For six days, the last thing they'd heard before dropping off to sleep and the first thing they'd heard waking up for work in the morning, was the incessant clatter of rain on the caravan roof.

Which made the silence that ushered in their day of rest seem at first almost eerie. The skies were still grey, but a lighter grey that slowly gave way to a grubby white, and by the time Ian set off on his own for the higher ground that was still to be weeded, a watery sun was starting to shine through brief gaps in the banks of cloud. Holiday or no, as he followed the muddy incline of what looked like a fairly clear furrow, it was second nature to him to take note of the positions and the density of those lush green patches of drenched bracken where some of the parallel rows of trees would disappear altogether, then reappear further up the slope. Nor could he stop himself from speculating how long it would take the four of them to weed that last part of the field and then move the caravan on to the next site.

Towards the brow of the hill the earth increasingly gave way to rocky outcrops that first deflected the regular rows of trees, then finally blocked their progress altogether, and from there Ian still had a steep scramble to reach the bald summit. Even so, he paused less to catch his breath than to mentally mark the borders of the ground yet to be cleared. Now that the last of the mist was evaporating, he could see for the first time the full extent of the area they'd already covered, and he roughly calculated that it shouldn't take them more than another day and a bit if they got back to it tomorrow. Then he'd allow himself a real holiday, however short, before he started the next contract.

Soon his gaze was drawn into the wider expanse of the long loch bending westwards through the hills, and beyond that he could even see the distant coastlines of the Inner Isles, all bathed in a tranquil summer light as the last wisps of cloud disappeared into the limitless blue. The unexpected radiance of the view persuaded him to take a seat amongst the rocks and boulders to eat his sandwiches and pour himself a coffee from the flask, and as he continued to absorb the panorama he was forced to admit he'd become near as dour and sullen as the weather itself over the past week. It was as if the constant rain had steadily seeped through his skin into his very soul, and if it had washed him clean, it had also left him more washed out than it was policy to let the rest of them detect.

Slowly his attention wandered back to the caravan, parked midway between the head of the loch and the hilltop, and at that distance he could clearly see the small bonfire round which the others' working clothes were still drying out on horizontal branches supported by upright ones hammered into the mud. Every so often a figure would emerge from the caravan to replace a dried pair of socks with a sodden tee-shirt or jeans, and when someone else picked their way across the makeshift stepping stones towards the burn, the visibility was now so good that Ian could easily make out the colour of the facecloth slapped across the shoulder.

As the muscles that had got used to holding his face stern against the rain began to relax at last, a wry smile replaced his frown as he listened to the yips and yelps of the others down below making ready for their raid on the village. For a moment, some similar yearning for adventure and romance – a yearning that had gone too long suppressed – swept over him, and there was still time to wave his hands in the air, shout *yee-haw* at the top of his voice and run back down the hill in his wellies to join them, even if that meant sitting in the open back of the pick-up all the way to the pub. After all, there was bound to be some ravishing young beauty there just waiting to be swept off her feet by an earthy forestry labourer–.

In his dreams.

He'd entertained such fantasies too often in the past to do anything these days but soberly realise it never happened that way. Watching the others throw the last of their dried clothes into the caravan, douse the fire and squeeze into the cab of his battered pick-up, Ian watched them make off for their pub lunch with the same steady smile on his face. All he hoped was that they'd remembered to take the shopping list as well as the money he'd advanced them for their work so far.

Then, quite abruptly, he turned his back on it all.

The far side of the hill dropped steeply down to the marshy floor of a narrow glen where the burn was still in spate, and on the lower reaches of the opposite slope a green band of fully-grown conifers basked in the sunshine like a complacent vision of the future. Without question the world would still exist in another thirty years, and without question that world would still want wood. And, by then, the new plantation he'd just turned his back on would be an almost exact replica of the one Ian looked at now: all ready for felling.

Beyond that, however, the resemblance ended. The upper limit of the mature woodland facing him was marked not by rocky outcrops, but by a firebreak and a deer fence. And on the further heights, where the heather and scrub rolled on out of sight, it was less the sudden presence of another figure in the landscape than the unusual clothes the woman wore that caught his attention. The headscarf, shawl and skirts – and what looked at that distance like a basket carried by her side – gave the impression that she'd emerged not only from the distant hills, but from another century.

Unobserved, he watched her half-run, half-stumble along the far side of the deer fence, stopping every so often to gaze at the unbroken length of it like some frustrated animal seeking richer pasture on the lower ground. All at once, she threw herself into a first attempt to scale the netting, only to be defeated by her cumbersome clothes. Soon the skirts and shawl had been cast aside on the heather, and from what now looked like a rucksack that she was carrying, out came a matching pair of black trousers and shirt that she quickly pulled on. In a desperate gambit, the rucksack itself was next pitched across the high fence, and after two more failed attempts the woman somehow managed to follow after it, falling heavily to earth on the other side.

There she lay for some time, either winded or injured, or both. Then, as Ian was about to quit his hiding place, she got up, loaded the pack on her shoulders, crossed the firebreak and disappeared into the wood, the direction of her downhill journey betrayed only by the black silhouettes of birds clawing up to wing as she passed.

Emerging at the foot of the glen and crossing the burn, it seemed she'd decided on heading for the very spot where he hid and, with the instinct of the hunter, Ian pressed himself even further under cover of the rocks.

Sure enough, she at last arrived, muddy-shoed and breathless, at a spot hardly twenty feet away. The sound of clinking metal as she dropped the rucksack to the ground seemed to remind her to untie the headscarf at last, and though her back was to him he distinctly caught the rich glint of silver as a couple of ornamental plates were pulled out of the pack, wrapped in the scarf to stop them making that jangling noise, and carefully replaced.

Now he could also see that the thick curve of hair that swept off her forehead down to her shoulders was black as her clothes – or black as the raven. For long before she turned round to scan the side of the hill where the caravan was parked, he could already feel that the proud, searching features of her face contained some vision of the land that was very different from his own. Whether or not it would prevail there was no way of telling: first the encounter itself must begin. But how? All he could think to do was to rise from his hiding place and, pointing a smiling finger at the slim curve of her belly, '*Bang*,' he said.

Her whole body spun towards him as if hit by the imaginary bullet, but she managed to stifle the cry that might instinctively have followed. Instead, she faced him so defiantly that the ironic smile vanished from his face, and before he knew it, he'd apologised for startling her. Wearily, she shrugged, yet he could feel the dark, dancing eyes continue to probe him from head to toe in an effort to decide how much of a threat he was. 'Does that track lead to a main road?' she wanted to know.

And though he told her that it eventually did, she seemed loath to proceed, as if some even more serious ambush might await her there. Finally she sat down on a boulder with the rucksack cradled protectively in her lap. 'What are you doing here?' she challenged him.

'Working on that plantation.' Ian hardly thought he needed to point it out, dressed the way he was.

'Is this still part of the estate?'

'Not as far as I'm aware. It's a forestry operation on this side of the fence.'

'And is that your caravan?'

'Yes. What exactly are *you* doing here?'

After a long pause, during which she seemed to match his story with his appearance and arrive at some provisional conclusion, the dark eyes focused directly on his own: 'I'm working for *Wildlife Freedom*.' Her grip on the rucksack tightened. 'I'm not a thief,' she insisted, although the charming smile she turned on him seemed far from genuine. 'Can I trust you?'

As he looked back at her, seriously pondering her question, Ian realised she must be in her early twenties, making her at least ten years younger than himself, and suddenly he felt less mature in her company than simply old. Pouring her a coffee from the flask, he eventually replied, 'You don't seem to have much choice.'

'I don't suppose I do.' She accepted the plastic cup with grace. Then, with the minimum statements required of any prisoner of war: 'I heard about the situation on the estate.' She offered him no further detail. 'It's being used for location shots by a film company today, so I got myself hired as an extra.' And she stopped there, as if that explained everything.

'But that stuff doesn't belong to you?' Ian nodded in the direction of her rucksack.

She ignored his question. 'I had to take the chance when I got it.'

He shared out the last of the coffee between them. 'So you made a run for it?'

She seemed to have decided the interrogation was over. Nodding sweetly, she made herself sound feminine again. 'Here I am.'

Ian suspected it was all a bit more serious than some student prank, but even if he chose to believe her wild romanticising, it still didn't help him make much sense of the whole thing. He could have cross-examined her further, but instead he sat there wondering what she planned to do next. No doubt she'd posed the same question herself if there was any truth in her story – which meant that she'd probably also calculated that the police might well be stopping cars on the main road by now. Suddenly, she was exercising her artificial charm to the utmost again. 'What would you say to me staying here until the whole thing blows over? I could help out, and you wouldn't need to pay me.'

It was all a far cry from any kind of adventure he'd ever set out on before, but he'd already told her she'd got herself a job before he realised that he'd arrived at his decision.

'Thanks,' she said, and this time he could have sworn her smile was genuine.

In the silence that followed, he could also have sworn that she allowed herself for the first time to see him as a man as well as some pawn in her game – and if he was right, he hoped she liked what she saw. A minute later, she was suggesting: 'Perhaps you could say I'm your girlfriend who's just turned up. If that won't compromise you.' And since none of the others knew him well enough to know whether that was true or not, he readily agreed. 'Your girlfriend's name is Marion, by the way.'

'Ian.' He shook the small hand that was offered to him, wondering how she would fare tomorrow with the sickle, for whatever strength she possessed must lie less in her arm than in her willpower. He then boldly kissed the smooth white back of the hand before releasing it. 'Just rehearsing.'

She gave no sign of being in the least distracted. Uppermost in her mind was the problem of where to hide the silverware, which she insisted on referring to as a ransom. But when she suggested the thick patch of bracken further down the hill, Ian could only shake his head: she obviously knew as much about forestry as he knew about filmmaking. Or *Wildlife Freedom* for that matter – he'd never heard of it. Was she making it all up? 'Tomorrow that bracken won't be there.' He explained that their job was to stop the saplings being choked by scything off the surrounding growth of weeds. So they decided instead on a hiding place right there beneath one of the boulders.

All ready to set off with him to the caravan, she asked if he had any food down there, only to hear that they were out of everything until the others got back from the village with fresh supplies. Yet all she did when he offered her his last uneaten sandwich was to prize it open suspiciously. 'Meat.' She handed it back to him. 'I can't eat that.' And when she saw his apologetic look of concern, she hissed,

'I'm hardly starving.' She glared at him so arrogantly that he strongly suspected she wouldn't have eaten it even if she was. 'Have you seen the deer?' She was now looking back towards the estate again, to the point where the fence disappeared over the horizon.

'None at all.'

Nodding in silent response she seemed to be making a supreme effort to control an anger so volcanic that it would willingly destroy the whole world in its existing form. 'Well, *that* –' she pointed at the hidden cache, 'is the only way I know of doing anything about it.'

By then, Ian had had enough of her obscure statements and her manic changes of mood, and he was glad to have a practical excuse to quit her company for a while. Handing her his box of matches in case she wanted to re-light the fire with the dry sticks from under the caravan, he left her to make her own way down and set off in the opposite direction to fetch the clothes she'd abandoned before anyone else came across them.

It didn't take him long to cross the glen and arrive at the deer fence, where his own difficulty scaling it in his heavy rubber boots somewhat renewed his respect for Marion, who was, after all, quite a few inches shorter. Her film costume remained where it had been cast off, and with no search parties in sight, he soon found himself walking with the bundle of clothes tucked under his arm to the spot she'd been gazing at earlier.

And there, where the fence dipped into a shallow gully, were the first red deer he'd seen that summer, about five or six of them, all in the initial stages of decay. Mostly they were hinds, but amongst the corpses two magnificent sets of antlers cut an even starker contrast to the thin, wasted limbs that had finally been able to support their weight no longer, the skinny forelegs already bruised and bloodied in what must have been some last forlorn attempt to break through the fence. No doubt they had found as little solace as Ian now did in the fact they had died not alone, but in each other's company. And most irreconcilable of all was the dead calf, curled up so neatly in the bony lap of a hind, the fur and sinew of its neck already scattered by the carrion.

The light breeze must have been behind him because he was suddenly startled by a movement some fifty yards further down the fence. A hind, with little more flesh on her than the dead bodies at his feet, limped off towards a distant patch of scrub so slowly that he felt he could easily have caught up with her at a medium trot. Turning his back on the scene, his own step became slower on the way home as he wordlessly fathomed the full depths of Marion's anger, and an eternity seemed to pass between catching sight of the re-kindled fire from the top of the hill and reaching it.

By then, her black trainers had been tied by their laces to the drying sticks, one on either side of her steaming socks, and she drew her feet back from the hot blaze before it flared up with the torn pieces of costume that Ian dropped on it. 'I'm sorry I've been so difficult.' The sentence had evidently been on her tongue for some time, awaiting his return. 'I do appreciate you sticking your neck out for me.'

'I understand your feelings about the deer.' It was all he could say. But it was enough to dispel the last of the tension that remained between them and allow them to sit together in the sunshine for however long it took before the sound of the pick-up in second gear announced its reappearance with Billy at the wheel, Kevin in the passenger seat, and no sign of the third member of the crew.

It turned out that the missing worker had been offered a lift back to town by some Glasgow holidaymakers they'd met in the pub, and when Ian heard the news he did no more than shrug. It had happened before; it would no doubt happen again. Some people simply couldn't handle the work – or the weather. Smiling his wry smile, he introduced them to his girlfriend Marion. 'I could see it coming, so I sent for a replacement.' Then he asked, as casually as possible, 'No trouble with the pick-up? One of the back tyres is getting a bit bald.'

'Can't be that bad,' Billy reckoned. 'We got stopped by the boys in blue on the way back and there was no hassle –'

'All they did was look under the tarpaulin,' Kevin chipped in, 'and then move us on. They must be looking for stolen goods, or someone on the run.'

'Or both,' Marion confidently added, for it was evident that neither of them had made any connection between the incident and her own arrival on the scene.

Soon she'd taken charge of unloading the supplies and volunteered to cook an evening meal (providing they didn't want meat with it), while Ian set about fixing a leak in the caravan roof. That left Billy and Kevin, both sadly disappointed with the lack of action in the village, to carry on working their way through the six-packs they'd brought back from the pub, and it didn't take them long to let Marion know they were going back to the city as soon as this job was finished and staying there. Then they continued to claim her attention with their tipsy talk for most of the evening.

At first, Ian was silently intrigued by how well she could give them the impression of an intimate exchange without revealing anything fundamental about herself – or her beliefs. But once the pink dusk had finally begun to fade, he could only control his impatience by setting himself the calming task of sharpening the sickles for the morning, clamping them one by one against the tailboard of the pick-up, where he could still work in the light of a moon that was almost full.

Whatever Marion eventually did to get rid of them, Billy and Kevin had staggered off to their sleeping berths in the caravan some time before he'd finished, and as he led her down to the burn to wash, he sensed some animal instinct had been stirring in his girlfriend too. After carefully brushing her teeth in the fast-flowing part of the burn, she stripped off her clothes and waded, soap in hand, to the deeper pool beyond, where she languidly watched Ian do the same. Perhaps it was all some kind of elaborate trap but, stiff with animal pride, he waded in to join with her.

In spite of the brilliant sunlight shining through the net curtains next morning, it was the latest they'd slept all week. Usually Ian gently roused the others with a strong cup of coffee, but that morning it was Marion with four un-matching bowls of porridge and strawberry jam who firmly insisted that they all wake up before it got cold.

Once the other three were out of the caravan and washed, Ian let them go on ahead while he quietly collected any items that could only belong to a woman – there were surprisingly few – and left them hidden in a plastic bag down by the burn. He'd already checked the previous day that there was no name on her rucksack, but for good measure he now decided to dump his shaving cream and razor in it before setting off. A few hundred yards up the hill he could see that Billy and Kevin had shown her the safe way to carry a sickle, and after the two musicians went off to work the topmost furrows, the only other thing was to demonstrate to Marion how the weeding itself was done.

At the tender age of three, most of the spruce were little over a foot high and, bending one of the saplings over to the ground, he quickly scythed off the surrounding weeds and then let it spring back upright again, unharmed. The main thing to avoid was accidentally snapping off the tops, but she soon got the hang of gripping them properly, and his only further advice was to stop if she lost her concentration. Otherwise she might chop a tree down twenty-five years prematurely, or lop off her toe instead of the weeds. And he wasn't insured against that, he warned her with a protective smile.

The first furrows that he gave her to check were clear enough for her to cover three or four rows at a time, working up to the point where Billy's and Kevin's patches began and then back down again, while Ian himself went off to tackle a stubborn patch on the lower border of the field. He'd long since begun to wonder whether he'd been over-cautious by the time the police car drew up alongside his pick-up, but once he saw one of the uniformed men reappear in the caravan doorway – having made his search, presumably – he was all ready to return the summoning wave with his own, shouting to Marion that he'd handle it.

Back down at base camp, he soon discovered that for a country bobby, the one in the moustache was not particularly friendly. Or particularly trusting. Even if his information had come from the forestry manager himself, he'd evidently seen fit to check it out against the berths, bags and backpacks in the caravan. 'Four of you?'

Ian turned his gaze back up the hill where the others were still working on. The combination of the heat and the wet had brought the midges out in their millions, and they'd all wrapped their heads in anything that would serve as a scarf before leaving the caravan, so he was pleased enough to see that Marion's long dark hair was as hidden from view as the others', and that Billy and Kevin looked no more like burly forestry labourers than she did. 'That's right.' He assumed a puzzled look. 'What's the problem?'

His question was disregarded. 'Have you seen anyone out on the hills?'

Ian allowed an expression of mild concern to replace the previous one. 'No. Has someone got lost?'

Slapping at the halo of midges round his head, the one with the moustache seemed eager to rejoin his partner, who continued to sit behind the wheel with the windows closed and a superior smile on his face. 'Never mind.' The bobby was shaking his head dismissively. 'She's probably long gone by now.' He walked off back to the shelter of the car, pausing only to give the back tyre of the pick-up an unpleasant kick: 'That's a problem, though.' He looked briefly over his shoulder. 'Get it changed.'

Ian felt strangely soothed by the idle thought that the sickle cradled in his arms was potentially an offensive weapon, but he stood silent and immobile while they reversed and left. Then he decided that the whole business was at an end at last, and back up the hill he went with sandwiches and coffee for everyone's lunch.

When Billy and Kevin anxiously reminded him about their band rehearsal back in Glasgow the following afternoon, he suggested that they could always work on into the evening, and get an early start tomorrow to finish it off. So on they worked until the light was starting to fade, and after working off their hangover while they were at it, the home comfort of Marion's evening meal made the musicians decide on the further comfort of an early night.

Long before that, Marion herself had already fallen so deeply asleep in front of the fire that she scarcely moved an exhausted muscle when her boyfriend carried her into her berth in the caravan, gently kissing her goodnight. And the last thing Ian heard before he kissed her again in his dreams was the familiar sound of rain drumming on the caravan roof.

If Marion seemed almost to relish the novelty of it, those last two soaking hours on the field the following morning broke the musicians' working spirit altogether. Ian could see them on the weeping horizon not bending any more, either feebly chopping at a bit of bracken here and there, or else suddenly attacking it with a furious swipe from the shoulder that was bound to hack down the trees along with the weeds. He'd never worked for this particular company before, so he could only hope that their part of the field would not be too closely inspected, and after they'd all finally called it a day and retreated to the shelter of the caravan he still had his fingers crossed when the forestry manager arrived mid-morning.

Ten days ago, Ian had assured him by telephone that his crew were all fully experienced, but with not so much as a proper set of waterproofs between the lot of them he strongly suggested they all stay out of sight in the caravan – not that they minded, not in the least – while he went out to meet the boss and tour the field with him. Half an hour later he was back with a cheque in his pocket, and if it was a case of getting ready cash for their final day and a bit, Billy and Kevin were quite agreeable to Ian making a solo journey into the village before they all left.

Once his cheque was in the bank, Ian felt a lot happier about replacing that back tyre while he was there, but the main reason for his trip was to see if the main road south would be clear of any spot-checks – it was – and to give Marion time to collect her 'ransom' from the top of the hill. All that remained to be done when he got back was to hitch up the caravan where his crew were still sheltering, and tow it to the site for the next contract, which the manager had marked on his O.S. map.

As the crow flew it was hardly a couple of miles away, but by caravan it would be nearer five. Slowly he drove down to the foot of the track where the torrents sweeping off the hills had again turned the roadside ditches into canals, and every dip of the road itself into a pond, forcing him to continue at a snail's pace through the rain until a gap at last appeared in the lavish growth of greenery that kept slapping on the windscreen. Somehow the pick-up managed to slither up an almost identical forestry track from there, but when he arrived at the new site and tried to reverse, the wheels spun uselessly in the mud. End of story.

In the short time it took the rest of them to tumble out of the caravan and help him push it into a stable position, wedging boulders under its retractable feet to make sure, they'd all got thoroughly soaked.

Again.

And still it continued to pour.

After Billy and Kevin had shared out the last of their dry

clothes between them and they'd all shared the last of the soup and the beans, Marion volunteered to be the first to ride in the open back of the pick-up on their way south. 'It's a lot worse for the deer,' was all she had to say in reply to their protests. So Ian gave her his waterproofs, making as comfortable a couch for her as he could with the sleeping-bags before she climbed in and he pulled the tarpaulin up round her waist, weighting it down at the sides with backpacks and rucksacks. Then Billy and Kevin made a dash from the caravan into the cab of the pick-up and away they went.

It was the first time the deer had been mentioned since they'd first met, and as he drove, Ian again found himself thinking what a hard winter it had been for them, with the wet spring and summer that followed sapping the last of their reserves. And then, thinking what a small part of the explanation that was for the scene they'd witnessed on the estate. There was no way the animals should have been left to starve. Even with their heads separated by the thick glass of the rear window, he could feel the rekindled heat of Marion's anger, caused perhaps by the brief glimpse they'd had of another section of that same deer fence, some distance up the hill from the new site.

Half an hour later Ian changed places with her, leaving Billy to take the wheel, and by the time Kevin's turn came the keyboard player had a relatively pleasant trip in the back of the pick-up winding down the side of Loch Lomond, where only a light drizzle fell on the islands and pleasure-boats. And when the red brick of the Alexandria tenements came into sight, they'd made good enough time to let the musicians pick up a chippie before their last short lap into the city, arriving outside their rehearsal hall ten minutes early. Even on the street they could hear the drummer who'd quit the country life a couple of days ago warming up on his kit, and as Marion helped to unload all their gear on to the pavement, Ian could feel the fast clip of the rock pattern accelerating them into the pace of city life.

As soon as Billy and Kevin had disappeared, she seemed to slam the cab door shut on the whole rural episode. 'Let's find Nick.' She gave Ian street-by-street directions over to the far side of the murky river, where eventually they parked outside an unremarkable tenement.

'Who's Nick?' Ian wanted to know as they climbed to the top floor.

'His father owns the estate. The whole thing was Nick's idea. Don't worry.' She was already hammering on the cartooned door. 'They can't stand each other.'

Soon the door was flung open and Marion was gripped in a bear hug by a strapping youth with a black brush of hair dividing his shaven head. His clothes were fashionably ripped, and when he eventually let go of her, Ian noticed that two of the rips had been pinned together with a large badge boasting the letter *A*. 'Welcome one and all.' Nick finally acknowledged Ian in a genteel tone that made his appearance seem even more bizarre.

As Marion told her tale in what looked like a shared kitchen in some student flat, Nick returned to his afternoon spliff with a widening grin on his face. 'Absolutely brilliant,' he complimented her as she reached the end of her narrative.

'So we're ready to do the negotiating,' she concluded. 'Once he feeds his animals he gets the family silver back – and we want proof. Photographs.'

'Absolutely brilliant,' Nick repeated. 'And you look totally the part, my man,' he complimented Ian next, offering him the smoke, which Ian didn't want.

Nor did Marion. 'Are you out your face again?' She started unbuckling the rucksack.

'Brilliant wind-up.' Nick was still babbling on. 'I almost believed you, I really did.' And then, as she finally displayed the trophies which proved her story beyond any shadow of doubt, Nick could only gape at her in stunned silence.

'Are you trying to tell me *you* were winding *me* up?' She was getting angrier by the minute.

Nick seemed mesmerised by his own distorted image in the plates. 'Aw, Marion,' he finally managed. 'If the old man ever hears I had anything to do with this…' He tailed off, shattered by this sudden threat to his lifestyle. 'He pays for my College course – and the flat. Everything,' he whined.

Marion's voice hardened as she stared him in the eye. 'So I'm going to have to do the negotiating myself?'

In the tense silence that followed, Ian noticed for the first time the intricate detail of the embossed family crests that decorated the plates, sitting there on the kitchen table under the strip-light, and he realised that Marion had been right to refer to them as ransom – they were far too distinctive to be sold. Perhaps Nick's racing thoughts had led him to a similar conclusion as a sly look eventually replaced the confusion on his face. 'I'll sort it out for you, Marion. Honest. I can say it was a student prank or something. Rag week – whatever.' Then came the veiled threat: 'I'll get them back to him and keep your name out of it. Nobody ever needs to know you were involved. I can keep my mouth shut.'

Marion seemed slow to realise how the tables had been turned on her, but as Nick's hands reached out to claim the plates, Ian was up off his chair, and both of them stopped there. If he'd been a betting man, Ian would have laid money on himself up against this upper crust mock Indian, and the odds seemed equally stacked on his girlfriend bursting not into tears but into fury. Maybe he should have been a betting man. *'You total waste of space.'* Marion grabbed the plates and hurled them full force against the kitchen wall, narrowly missing Nick's shoulder in the process. *'You total time-waster, and the deer are dying all the time.'* And without another wasted word she stormed out, seemingly oblivious to Ian's very existence.

The smoke in the ashtray had long since died through lack of attention, and before Ian went chasing after his girlfriend the last he saw of Nick was a bent figure kneeling on the kitchen floor desperately trying to straighten out a severely buckled rim.

Marion was draped round a lamp-post further down the street when he caught up with her, the flood of fury now all too predictably replaced by a flood of tears. She put up no resistance when he wrapped her in his arms. 'You have a good heart, Marion,' he told her over and over, like some mantra that might finally sort it all out, and gradually it seemed to work: the sobbing slowly subsided. He realised that it was long past time he took control of things again, and when he told her they both needed to eat, she meekly agreed.

He had enough money in his pocket for them to dine out just about anywhere in the whole city, but neither of them was dressed for anywhere classy, so they ended up in the nearest chippie that had a café attached to it. Marion parked herself and her rucksack behind a formica-topped table while Ian stopped at the counter to place their order. Then he sat down opposite her. 'You've got to stop giving yourself such a hard time.' He was trying to keep his voice both quiet and firm. 'You're a very attractive woman.' And, sensing he hadn't gone far enough: 'A very beautiful woman.'

She sat there in silence as the tea arrived in two thick china mugs along with white triangles of bread, thriftily spread with a pale margarine. 'There are other ways you could help the animals,' he began, because he'd been giving it quite a lot of thought on the drive down to the city. And after the waitress had dumped their macaroni pie suppers on the table and disappeared again through the arch, he went on to tell her about the small piece of land that was attached to the farm cottage he rented. He had no plans for it and he couldn't see his landlord objecting to something legitimate – like an animal sanctuary, maybe?

But she showed no interest in even taking a look at the place, and they finished their meal in silence. Only the fate of the deer seemed to move her. 'They should have been fed,' she said quietly as she laid her cutlery down on her empty plate.

'They should have been culled.' Ian decided to set her straight once and for all, because he knew what he was talking about – even if it might be a long time before he could admit it to his girlfriend. Long before he'd become his own boss, the deer cull had been an occasional part of his job (for there was no denying that the animals' eating habits could severely damage a forest) and none of his fellow marksmen had relished the task any more than he had. But there was no other way. The best that could be accomplished was a quick, clean kill.

'They should have been fed,' she repeated.

'It's no long-term solution,' he countered. 'A certain amount of land can only support a certain number of animals.'

'And does that apply to our own species as well?'

Marion stomped off to the *Ladies*, leaving him to idly speculate how many hundreds of thousands of humans inhabited how many square miles of concrete, tarmac and the occasional patch of grass that surrounded them. And what perverse laws of nature could conceivably make it all possible. Lost in his thoughts while he waited for her to come back, Ian even began to wonder whether it might have been something wild and free within himself that he'd been required to kill those many years ago …

A warm pair of hands gently blindfolded him, and he felt a soft kiss planted on the top of his head. 'Let's go back to the caravan,' Marion whispered in his ear. Then the blindfold was removed so her hands could start massaging his shoulder blades. 'Things were good between us there.'

'That's what you want to do?'

'Yes.' She went back to her side of the table to collect the rucksack.

Ian needed to make some phone calls to find a replacement crew for the next contract, but he could as easily do that from the village tomorrow. Besides, he'd told her he was taking some time out after finishing that last marathon, and he meant it. 'Do you need to pick up some stuff first?' He thought he would at least find out where she lived, even if she wasn't inviting him to stay there.

Marion shook her head. 'I can buy anything I need.'

And all she needed for that was a cash-line point, so Ian once again found himself in tow to her latest whim. Not that he minded. Its romantic appeal was still firmly rooted in the tingling afterglow in his shoulder blades as they went on to laugh their way through a supermarket, loading whatever took their fancy into the shopping trolley. And then off again into the wilds, stopping only once at a camping site along the way for a shower and to fill the plastic water bottles, because Ian hadn't noticed any running water in the vicinity of the new site.

It was late evening when they got there, and the rain was still holding off, but the moon (which must surely be full by now) was still hidden behind banks of undulating cloud, leaving them to unload their supplies in a soft half-light. The caravan was cluttered with tools which they'd parked there before they left, so they decided to open up some more space by moving them back into the pick-up. 'What's this giant spade thing?' Marion wanted to know after she'd manoeuvred it out through the caravan door.

'It's a right-handed rutter.' Ian gave it its full name, amused at her theatrical attempts to use it like an ordinary spade. 'That's not how it works.' He helped her to tilt it instead to a forty-five degree angle, which transformed the flat metal pedal on the top right of the blade into a more obvious footrest.

'So?' She still hadn't figured it out.

'So you pedal, and cut the side of a ditch with it.' He took over with a practical demonstration. 'Eighteen inches deep and eighteen inches wide. Someone else follows up with a shovel. Or a spade.'

'And these?' Her interest had already shifted to the long-handled snips which Ian kept handy in case they hit any old buried fencing that would blunt the rutter blade.

'Giant scissors,' he laughed, secretly pleased that she wanted to know more about the ditching, which was likely to be part of the next contract. He was still hoping she'd take him up on his offer of staying on here, and he'd already planned to set up a tent for them both so they could get a bit of mutual distance from the rest of the new crew, whoever they might turn out to be.

But tonight the two of them had the caravan all to themselves. After Marion had replaced the snips on top of the other tools in the large wooden box and they'd both hoisted it into the back of the pick-up, Ian pulled down the tarpaulin – just to be on the safe side, because there was no telling how long the current dry spell would last, even if the clouds had now parted to reveal a full white orb of moon. It left enough room inside the caravan for Marion to draw all the curtains without contorting herself, and she lit some candles instead of the smelly paraffin lamp before they undressed and cuddled into the bunk that was Ian's.

It began slowly, not like it had been that first wild night in the burn. This time she seemed to be challenging him to apply the same steady perseverance that he showed in his work to their mutual pleasure, and he responded with all the physical reserves he had left, resisting every temptation to stop before the job was finally completed, down to the last delicious detail. And with a blind trust that he'd be paid in full by his girlfriend falling eternally in love with him, he'd long since fallen into a deep, deserved sleep in his narrow bunk by the time Marion blew out the candle stubs and slipped quietly away to her own berth at the door end of the caravan.

A little before morning, Ian had a dream not remotely like any dream he'd ever had before. He was roaming the wilds at the mercy of the elements, directed not by anything he saw, but by an acute sense of smell and hearing. All the scents and sounds that engulfed him had their own immediate meaning: some were neutral, others warned of danger, and others still drew him on to richer pastures He could feel the ground below him, and the change from mud to rock to heather, but his movement across it was so effortless that he was aware of it only through the changes in the composition of the hills, the lochs, the glens and the woods that surrounded him, and the changing position of the sun. And all the time that these animal messages entering through his ears and nostrils were being spontaneously translated into action, he could feel another presence by his side: some kindred animal spirit responding as he responded, taking nourishment when he did, sheltering where he sheltered – even ducking for cover when he did. Together they moved in a timeless synchronicity over a vast and boundless territory that had always been their own …

He almost woke up around dawn, but the thick curtains confused his sense of time, and an inescapable desire to return to his dream soon dragged him back down to unconsciousness. So it was almost noon before he finally surfaced, his whole body totally refreshed. Sitting in the doorway of the caravan, he vaguely wondered where Marion had disappeared to, but he wasn't too bothered. She'd probably realised how much he'd needed the rest and had gone for a walk on her own, as the footprints that led up the hill suggested. So Ian made himself a leisurely coffee before he followed the trail, undecided about whether he was more pleased that it wasn't raining or that he wasn't going to work today.

Hardly had he set off than he could have sworn he caught some movement on the periphery of his vision, but when he turned in that direction there was nothing to be seen. His instinct was to walk more quietly after that, which allowed him to catch a brief glimpse of two deer grazing in the wood before they also quickly disappeared. He couldn't understand how they'd got there – this was the forestry side of the fence. And surely the fence itself must be fairly close by now, if his sense of direction was correct?

He was partly right. The next curve in the track revealed a regular line of posts, but the shredded, tangled netting hanging limply between them could hardly be called a fence any more, and the wreckage continued as far west as the eye could see. Ian stared in disbelief, resisting the explanation for it with every bone in his body. This could be his whole living on the line. His reputation. Even his freedom – how could he have been as crazy as she surely was?

And all at once, he was running back down the track to the caravan with all the speed and accuracy he'd had in his dream, and when he discovered that Marion's rucksack was gone from under her bunk, the howl that rose up from his innards was scarcely human. Then he found himself tearing the tarpaulin off the back of the pick-up and flinging open the lid of the toolbox. The snips had been neatly replaced on top of the pile and she'd obviously found the packet of chalks as well. Scrawled on the inside of the wooden lid was a single word: *BANG*.

AFTERWORD

A View of the Stories

The *Balintore Writers' Group* met fortnightly, and the bus from
Tain arrived early, leaving me enough time to take a walk down
to the harbour pier and draw a bracing breath of sea air before
the afternoon session began. Although Community House was a
wood-faced building identical to all of its neighbours in the small
housing development, the name-plate made it easy to find. It soon
became a home from home: just the right size to host half a dozen
writers round a living-room table, with tea and coffee on tap in the
kitchen and, more often than not, some home baking brought in
by one of the group.

On my first visit I was diplomatic enough to place myself last
on the list of readers, and the response – including my own – to
what was read was so animated that the session was over before my
own turn arrived. Everyone was extremely apologetic, but I wasn't
the least bit sorry myself. The slick and cynical *let-it-burn* prose of
my bachelor years wasn't even pleasing me any more, so there was
no reason to suppose it would please the present company either.
Since becoming a parent I'd become much more concerned with
the kind of world that we're passing on to the next generation – but
my writing hadn't yet caught up with that change of outlook.

At that first session I'd been particularly affected by the pieces
that Bess and Dolly had read. Although Bess was writing fiction
and Dolly was writing local history (documenting customs and
traditions which might otherwise be lost with the passing of time)
they both wrote exactly the way they spoke – and that was what I
needed to hear.

On my second visit I was able to get away with reading a couple
of tried-and-tested performance pieces from my Edinburgh days,
but by then I was already working on *The Crash*, which was to be
the story – or at least *a* story – of industrial development in Easter
Ross. It seemed that the local idiom itself must have been as much
affected by this development as any other aspect of life here, and

the phrase 'Industrial Gaelic' kept popping into my head – even if I couldn't pin down exactly what it meant.

Something else that had intrigued me for a long time was Joseph Conrad's unusual use of the first person plural narrative in one of his novels, and now it seemed that I could legitimately steal this approach for my own story. My narrator would tell the tale not as an individual but as a member of a community, because in this part of the world community was still a lot more than something the government sent you a bill for belonging to.

There were lots of big themes spinning round in my head, like the boom-crash cycle of capitalism, and the question of what had happened to socialism in this country. Was it still alive? Had it been murdered? Had it committed suicide? I even decided to imply that Alec was a descendant of legendary labour leader John Maclean. But I wasn't writing propaganda: nothing was to take priority over the unfolding story of Alec and Shona.

The next time that I took the bus to Balintore *The Crash* was completed and I met Aonghas, a large and friendly Gael who was Writer-In-Residence for Ross & Cromarty at the time. Like Sorley Maclean, he would read his verse first in the original Gaelic, then in his own translation, and it was music to the ear in both versions. Sometimes he would chat to Dolly in the Gaelic during breaks, but only long enough for them both to indulge their love of the language and not so long as to exclude the rest of us. Aonghas liked *The Crash*, as did Bess and Dolly, but the most reassuring response came from another member of the group who swore that the story recounted exactly how it had been for her husband and herself when they first came to the area. She also found it hard to believe I'd never worked at Nigg myself, but that I'd simply listened to a lot of people who had.

I took the bus back to Tain with a distinct feeling that I was finally working along the right lines, but uppermost in my mind was an interesting story I'd heard from Dolly about a plane crash near Loch Eye some years previously...

Elizabeth Sutherland's fascinating book about the second sight, *Ravens and Black Rain*, had already interested me in the fictional possibilities of the theme. It was there I learned that if seers don't happen to be in anyone else's company at the time, they're quite likely to forget the future they've just witnessed. Fortunately, I remembered that particular piece of information long enough for it to become a vital part of my next plot.

Ravens and Black Rain also includes a detailed biography of Swain Macdonald, our local seer, who lived about six miles up the road, near Edderton. Swain had become as much of a local feature as the standing stones themselves, but when some relatives of my fiancée who were up here on holiday invited me along with them to hear what my future held, I had to decline. I was already mentally constructing my own fictional seer as an idealised version of my grandfather, and I didn't want any confrontation with reality to knock me off course. (It remains one of my regrets, because Swain unfortunately passed away soon afterwards and I never did get to meet him.)

Researching Dolly's story in Inverness Library, I eventually tracked down a brief account of the aeroplane accident in *The Times,* after drawing a blank with the microfiche records of all the local newspapers. While I was at it, I thought I might as well find out what the weather had been like that particular day, and that was enough to get the story off to its meandering start. All the jigsaw pieces of the plot were fitting together, and the only foreseeable problem was convincing the reader that John Mackenzie had picked up at least a layperson's knowledge of quantum physics along the way.

It was evident to me by then that Bess and Dolly had preserved a more rural lilt to their writing than the 'Industrial Gaelic' of *The Crash,* and the new subject matter of *The Seer* seemed to offer an opportunity to try to imitate their style more closely. Although the narrator would never formally introduce himself, he would most likely be of the same generation and background as John Mackenzie himself, and so he could tell the story as they would.

As before, big themes occupied my thoughts. Centuries-old questions, like free will and predestination, and the values that are worth living by. But, once again, fiction had to come first. The dramatic focus had to remain on the developing relationship between the two men.

Looking back on these first two stories now, *The Crash* seems overly pessimistic if it does indeed imply that socialist awareness died along with Alec – but, equally, *The Seer* seems overly optimistic in its implication that Richard Britten could be redeemed. That particular character – or, perhaps more accurately, caricature – was originally designed to embody many of the less savoury aspects of Thatcherite man. But is New Labour man essentially any different?

Some questions can only be left with the reader, and of course your answers will always depend on your own particular perspective. Meanwhile, I already had a title for what I could foresee as a collection of stories that would ask a few further questions, but that would somehow also belong together, if only in the act of questioning itself: *Highland Views.*

That irksome phrase 'Industrial Gaelic' still wouldn't go away, and I still didn't know what it meant – particularly the Gaelic part. I didn't speak or understand a word of the language, much as I enjoyed the music of it. But perhaps that was the vital clue: the music of it.

Yes, the language of subversion had been officially outlawed after the suppression of the second Jacobite rebellion. And yes, Gaelic did persist nonetheless in parts of the country where the law was not enforced, or not enforceable. But what about the Highland speakers who adopted (or had been forced to adopt) the King's English? The answer suddenly came to me: they hadn't. They'd juggled the words of this new language in any way they pleased, as long as it preserved the old speech rhythms. You could still hear it down the street. 'It's cold out the day, right enough' means exactly the same as 'It's certainly cold outside today,' but the underlying rhythms are completely different.

Of course this was all pure speculation, but I found the idea intoxicating. It was possible – at least indirectly – to draw on the rich heritage of Gaelic rhythm without having to abandon the language I'd learned from birth. It also meant that I didn't need to don the mask of a narrator any more: I could write directly, and in a style of my own making. And that was the only way to approach the next story.

The theme of Scottish independence was in the air then as it is now, but at the time of writing the 'ethnic cleansing' that preceded the formation of new 'independent' nation-states in the Balkans was more recent history. And so it seemed essential that for the good of the vast majority of us, the matter of 'ethnicity' and the matter of 'sovereignty' should be kept separate, and not made into an explosive mix by manipulative politicians. After all, taking a long historical view, today's natives are generally yesterday's incomers.

And so the heroine of *A Lament For The Union* could not be of Highland, or even of Scottish, origin.

It hadn't taken life long to catch up with fiction, because by then I *was* working at Nigg, on tanker-duty nightshifts as part of a twelve-man crew based in a Portacabin near the pier. (Ships would usually take two or three days loading oil, and our duty was to take fast action in the event of fire or spillage.) I was also working part-time for the *Highlands Music Centre* and running a Writing Workshop for the Community Support Group in Tain, so it was becoming increasingly difficult to keep in regular contact with the group in Balintore.

It was the same for Bess. Her first-ever story had won the first-ever Neil Gunn competition, and Aonghas had helped her to find a publisher for a book. But the book would have to be double the length of her existing collection, which usually left her too busy writing to come along to discuss writing – a highly enviable predicament, I couldn't help but think at the time. Aonghas had also been busy organising a series of *Words And Music* events with visits from well-known Scottish writers, and he would usually invite either Bess or myself to represent local writing. It was a great opportunity to meet and learn from the professionals and to test our stories out on a larger audience – and to hear some fine *clarsach* playing. But, however busy we were, we always tried not to miss any of the ceilidhs that Dolly regularly organised in the Balintore Hotel, because they were something else again.

When Aonghas couldn't get to Balintore, Bill had been our afternoon's host, responsible for opening up Community House and locking it up again when we were done. He was also involved with the *Writers North* group, and he'd issued an open invitation to us all. So once I'd passed my driving test and got an old banger on the road, it was easier to get to the evening meetings at Bill's house, for putting me in touch with *Two Ravens Press*. Sharon, its editor, already knows how much I appreciate the leeway that she's given me by not insisting on including additional material which doesn't belong here, small as the final book may be.

Clio Gray has assisted me way beyond the call of duty on many different fronts in Tain Library. And, finally, I must also thank my dear friend Linda for all those impromptu tutorials in word-processing and for formatting the final manuscript.

May this *Year of Highland Culture* bring a return to the spirit of Dolly's ceilidhs, where poets and storytellers would recite, musicians would play and dancers would dance, all for the love of it.

David Ross
January 2007

Recent Titles from Two Ravens Press

Titles Published in April 2007

Love Letters from my Death-bed.
Cynthia Rogerson
The adventures of a Scottish bigamist dying – or is she? – in California. There's something very strange going on in Fairfax. Joe Johnson is on the hunt for dying people while his wife stares into space and flies land on her nose; the Snelling kids fester in a hippie backwater and pretend that they haven't just killed their grandfather; and Morag, multi-bigamist from the Scottish Highlands, makes some rash decisions when diagnosed with terminal cancer by Manuel – who may or may not be a doctor. Meanwhile, the ghost of Consuela threads her way through all the stories, oblivious to the ever-watching Connie – who sees everything from the attic of the Gentle Valleys Hospice.
£8.99; ISBN 978-1-906120-00-9

Highland Views. David Ross
Military jets exercise over Loch Eye as a seer struggles to remember the content of his vision; the honeymoon is over for workers down at the Nigg yard, and an English incomer leads the fight for independence both for Scotland and for herself … This debut collection of short stories from a gifted writer provides an original perspective on the Highlands, subtly addressing the unique combination of old and new influences that operate in the region today.
£7.99; ISBN 978-1-906120-05-4

Castings. Mandy Haggith
A collection of poems by Mandy Haggith, whose writing clearly reflects her love for the land and her concern for the environment – not just in the North-West Highlands where now she lives on a woodland croft, but in her travels around the world.
£8.99; ISBN 978-1-906120-01-6

Riptide: New Writing from the Highlands and Islands. Edited by Sharon Blackie and David Knowles
A collection of microfiction, short stories and poetry by writers from the Highlands and Islands – established writers and names to watch. Includes contributions by Andrew Greig, Cynthia Rogerson, John Glenday, Angus Dunn and many others.
£8.99; ISBN 978-1-906120-02-3

Titles Forthcoming in July 2007

Types of Everlasting Rest: a collection of short stories from Scotsman-Orange Prize Winner and novelist Clio Gray
ISBN 978-1-906120-04-7
The Language of It: a poetry collection by Stephen Watts
ISBN 978-1-906120-03-0
Leaving the Nest: a poetry collection by Dorothy Baird
ISBN 978-1-906-120-06-1
Nightingale: a novel by Peter Dorward
ISBN 978-1-906-120-09-2

Titles are available direct from the publisher at
www.tworavenspress.com, or from any good bookshop.

Two Ravens Press Ltd., Green Willow Croft, Rhiroy, Lochbroom, Ullapool IV23 2SF. Tel. 01854 655307